THE
COMPLETE
LITTLE ONES

GAVIN EWART

By the same author
Poems and Songs, 1939
Londoners, 1964
Pleasures of the Flesh, 1966
The Deceptive Grin of the Gravel Porters,
    1968
The Gavin Ewart Show, 1971
Be My Guest! 1975
No Fool Like An Old Fool, 1976
The First Eleven, 1977
Or Where a Young Penguin Lies
    Screaming, 1978
All My Little Ones, 1978
The Collected Ewart 1933–1980, 1980
The New Ewart (Poems 1980–1982), 1982
More Little Ones, 1982
The Ewart Quarto, 1984
The Young Pobble's Guide to his Toes,
    1985

THE
COMPLETE
LITTLE ONES

GAVIN EWART

His Shortest Poems

Hutchinson

London Melbourne Auckland Johannesburg

© Gavin Ewart 1986

First published in 1986 by Hutchinson & Co
(Publishers) Ltd

An imprint of Century Hutchinson Limited
Brookmount House, 62–65 Chandos Place,
London WC2N 4NW

Century Hutchinson Publishing Group
(Australia) Pty Ltd
16–22 Church Street, Hawthorn, Melbourne,
Victoria 3122

Century Hutchinson (NA) Ltd
32–34 View Road, PO Box 40–086, Glenfield,
Auckland, 10

Century Hutchinson Group (SA) Pty Ltd
PO Box 337, Bergvlei 2012, South Africa

Set in 11 on 12pt Palatino

Printed and bound in Great Britain by
The Guernsey Press Co. Ltd, Guernsey,
Channel Islands

ISBN 0 09 167311 9

Miss Twye was soaping her breasts in her bath
When she heard behind her a meaning laugh
And to her amazement she discovered
A wicked man in the bathroom cupboard.

New Verse, 1938

Introduction

With the addition of sixty-seven new poems (Extra
Little Ones) to the contents of *All My Little Ones* and
More Little Ones, this volume contains all the short
poems I have thought fit to 'preserve'.

Mostly, they are concerned with hypocrisy –
particularly as this affects our attitudes to sex – and
to a lesser extent with the pseuds of the literary world.

Some have appeared in the following publications
(and to them acknowledgments are due): *Ambit,
Encounter, Light Year 1986* (U.S.A.), *London Magazine,
New Directions 33* (USA), *New Statesman* (competition
entries), *Oxford Poetry, Quarto, Thames Poetry, The
Honest Ulsterman, The Listener, The Little Word Machine,
The London Review of Books, The Times Literary
Supplement, Tribune, Tuba*; also the cricket anthology
Summer Days, edited by Michael Meyer.

Let nobody despise these little poems because they
are short, or seem trivial. Even a great genius like
William Blake was content to write such verse:

> When a Man has married a Wife, he finds out whether
> Her knees and elbows are only glued together.

Part I

ALL MY LITTLE ONES

HAIL AND FAREWELL

The sick Get Well Card simply says Drop Dead!

DOUBLE HAIKU: BRITAIN AND SURREALISM

Since we live in a
country where shops sell German
Juice and Big Choosy

Cat Food, where they say
'She laughed like a drain!', we just,
really, don't need it.

FOLK-HERO

The one the foreign students call Ted Huge.

VARIATION ON A POMPEIAN BROTHEL GRAFFITO

I like a girl with a big black mat
(worth a serenade, a song, or a sonnet)
between her legs – but in addition to that
it's got to have WELCOME written on it.

NEGATIVE

A landlady is not a countrywoman

A *mariage blanc* is not a white wedding

A planchette is not a ghost writer

A sperm whale is not a Don Juan

An *oeil de boeuf* is not a bullseye

A mons veneris is not the Venusberg

A peccary is not a serious sin

SIMULATION/STIMULATION

A sex film that doesn't show a male erection
is really cheating;
it's like showing gourmets at a banquet
and not showing what they're eating.

CREATION MYTH HAIKU

After the First Night
the Sun kissed the Moon: 'Darling,
you were wonderful!'

HAIKU: THE SEASON OF CELEBRITY

With summer comes the
bluebottle; with pleasant fame
comes the journalist.

EDWARDIAN HAIKU: SCRUBBERS

Women scrubbing floors –
high ladies in this posture
admitted lovers.

THE SURREALIST LANDSCAPE

A huge can of soup is walking the pavement

The evening oleanders are softly barking

All over the world the sea turns orange

A fish-headed man makes love to a woman

The cats all, suddenly, have six legs

The roses, of course, are smelling of seaweed

A giant hand in the sky makes the thumbs-down sign

THESE WERE THE NAMES OF THE NOVELS

A Wine Called Albert

The Witty Young Friends

The Sex-Benders

Nobody Wants Me

Mrs Gentry And The Basilisk

The Perfumed Sinner

Come And Get It!

THE RHYMING SLANG OF THE POSTCARDS

If she sends you a duck
she wants a fuck

If she sends you a hearse
she's got the curse

If she sends you a ship
she's taking a trip

If she sends you a bed
she means 'Drop dead!'

THE ALLITERATIVE LAMENT

Those who laughed have been laid low

Those who kissed have been killed

Those who sang have been slaughtered

Those who danced have been done away with

Those who loved have been liquidated

Those who smiled have been smitten

Those who exulted have been exterminated

THE CHARACTERS THAT MADE THE PLAYS SO MARVELLOUS

Old Doghope in *The Thriving Wives of Swivedom*

Red Knob in *Lust!*

Lord Catchpenny in *The Devil To Pay*

Lady Mantrap in *The Provoking Misunderstanding*

The Graf von Tippfehlern in *Die Ausstreicherin*

Miss Petticoat in *The Great Value of Underwear*

Alice B.Agony in *It All Begins At Sunset*

SEASONAL DOUBLE HAIKUS: THE MATING SEASON

1 The young man, naked,
  lies with the girl impaled on
  his cock. She's smoking.

  They move, very slow,
  it's like something under the
  sea, so beautiful.

2 The girl says 'How do
  you want me? On my hands and
  knees?' He arranges

  her. This is what the
  Victorians always called
  'unnatural vice'.

3 The little Jewish
  girls have small wet cunts that taste
  of gefilte fisch,

  they wriggle so, so
  happily, under lovers'
  probing, tickling tongues.

FORM

If
I
wrote
it
all
out
like
this
(the
way
the
amateurs
do
and
the
conceited
zeros)
I
should
kill
myself
with
boredom
!

THE BEGINNING OF AN AUGUSTAN ODE TO MASTURBATION, WRITTEN AT THE REQUEST OF SEVERAL LADIES AND GENTLEMEN OF QUALITY

Oh, Masturbation! Lord of Kings and Queens,
That from our Cradle bring'st us such Delight,
               By Day and by Night
Tho' unconfess'd, the Master of Us All,
That hold'st this Realm in Thrall,
And hast so many Modes and untold Means!

THE 1930s SEX NOVEL

She undid his uniqueness
and tickled his twosome.

DOUBLE HAIKU: THE LOST COMPOSITIONS

Haydn's 'Hen', yes. But
we've lost his 'Caterpillar',
his 'Sheep' and his 'Goat',

and, of Beethoven's,
his 'Mosquito Symphony',
his noble 'Frog March'.

A DAISYCHAIN FOR THE QUEEN'S JUBILEE (1952–77)

Unique queendom! Mother! Renew
wives, sons, sad daughters!
So only yesterday you, undaunted,
dedicated, dominating, gave
easily your royal love endlessly,
yes, set the ethnic crown nobly
yet tremulously yours!
Simple earned devotion now will
lessen newly your real, lived,
dumb burden. Now we elevate
emotional loud delighting
garish high hymns solemnly!
Yours soundly! Yours serenely!

Note

The Daisychain was invented by my wife in the Spring of 1977, when she suggested that I should write a poem where each word began with the last letter of the word before. Perhaps 'unique queendom' is stretching this rule a bit, but the principle is there.

HAIKU: HELL'S GRANNIES

Och! Women Old Age
Pensioners, clogging Post Off-
ices! (I'm eighteen).

EARLY TRIBES

Primitive prickmen
lustfully levering
the weight of women
fucking the fatness

WINTER HAIKU (EXPANDED)

Filling hot water bottles
with a plastic funnel, I think of
Mme de Brinvilliers' water torture.

A SHORT HISTORY OF RENAISSANCE ROME

Popes full of sex and simony

THE POOR RICH

They're eating crippled strawberries, wounded beef.
Why, everything they eat is dead!
The vegetables die as they are pulled,
they give up their roots like ghosts,
beheaded cabbages, desperate potatoes
longing to propagate, the blood of those tomatoes
is acid for them! All fish is fish-veal,
blood-emptied, colourless.

Pigs bleed to death – they eat the rending scream.

WOMEN'S WORK

The moony womby poems that taste of blood.

PATRONAGE

With a wry smile they wheeled out the inflatables
to inspire a community sense in the dogshit streets.

INVASION

Is it not passing brave to be a king
and charge in arabhood through Selfridges?

THE NATIONAL GAMES

The main event was Throwing The Jelly Baby

Sideshows included Runes and Tongue-twisters

One bardic exercise was Travelogue in Trochees

There was a Competitive Dash to the National Dish

Strange music was made on a one-stringed instrument

Racial Dancing got combined with Rounders

They drank till dawn from The Cup of Hatred

THE CRITICS AND THE GOLDEN AGE

'the life-giving importance'

'a master of hyperbole'

'the mystery embodied over against them'

Like ash and volcanic mud

on Pompeii and Herculaneum

time and death fall

on Putney and Hurlingham

RUGBY SPECIAL CLERIHEW

Damaroids
help tired old men with haemorrhoids –
but, in sober truth,
the best aphrodisiac is Youth.

T. STURGE MOORE

When I was young
I found T. Sturge Moore
a very boring poet –
but now that I am old
I find him even more boring still.

PENAL

The clanking and wanking of Her Majesty's prisons.

JOHN REGINALD HALLIDAY CHRISTIE

'The same stone which the builders refused: is become the head-stone
in the corner.'—PSALM CXVIII

So the man who was once called
'Can't Do It Christie'
and 'Reggie-No-Dick'
by disappointed girls in Halifax,
rose to be the greatest sex-maniac
of his generation.

LIFE-STYLE

The farmyard squeals in the breakfast bacon

The sun is shining in the noble vintage

The eggs are clucking in the honourable omelette

The wheat is windswept in the loaves we love so

In the beefburgers the bulls are bellowing

The peat-clean water wobbles through the whisky

The calmness of cows murmurs in the milk

ON THE 'A' LEVEL SYLLABUS

Running-Dogs of Power by C. P. Smog

Selected Short Tories by W. D. & H. O. Wills
(includes Lord Piglet)

Cock Rise to Candlewick
(old-time wife-swapping in Outer Suburbia)

The Duchess of Murphy by Sean O'Webster
(impact of the Troubles on a Ducal household)

Rory O'Lanus by Patrick MacShakespeare
(the stirring drama of Celtic and Rangers)

Selected Perms by W. Money

THE LITTLE PICTURES

A refined old lady cries 'Oh, crosswords!' when she
drops a stitch

A madman tries to cut his throat with an electric razor

A man in tweeds and a cap says 'The summer is still
with us!'

A girl in a sweetshop is vacant. 'Cruncher? I've never
heard of Cruncher!'

An impresario describes a new kind of cricket, played
on bicycles

Secret Service memoirs: 'The prettiest thing I ever set
spies on!'

Kneeling Poet Laureate presents an *Ode To Sex* to the
Queen

IMPACTED

There was a young lady of Penge
who was killed when a stone at Stonehenge
with great force and no sound
drilled her into the ground.
So sad a death none can avenge!

THE DIFFERENCE

The difference between churches and factories
everyone understands –
it's the difference between the laying on
and the laying off of hands.

HAIKU: AFTER THE ORGIES

All the Maenads had
terrible hangovers and
unwanted babies.

TWO NONSENSE LIMERICKS

Nonsense Limerick i

Eggwood limestone filbert horse
prayerbird angel trefoil gorse
tabard tunic
writing runic
semaphore semaphore morse!

Nonsense Limerick ii

Cathedral, amphetamine, string,
annuity, edelweiss, ling,
indemnity, cheese,
alabaster, demise,
ululate, underestimate, sing!

THOUGHT ABOUT THE HUMAN RACE

We are just a passing smile on the face of Venus.

DOWNFALL

the
ass

    yri
    anc

        ame
        dow

            nli
            kea

                wol
                fon

                    the
                    fol

                        d.

SERIOUS SONG

Elitist people
are the sweetest people
that one could ever know,
they're really choosy,
quite sincerely choosy,
they prefer Shakespeare to any
two-a-penny, jumped-up, bumped-up
illiterate so-and-so!

THE OLD-FASHIONED EPIGRAM

Her face was old and drawn –
and then it was carefully painted.

A GREAT POEM

This is a great poem.

How I suffer!
How I suffer!
How I suffer!

This is a great poem.
Full of true emotion.

ORDINARY

Ordinary poems for ordinary people
is an ordinary poet's dream.
This sounds like a moderate wish – but always
the ordinariness is extreme!

ODD MEN OUT, STATESIDE

Micky, Dicky, Ricky and Licky
played Randy Roulette with Bernadette, Colette
and Nanette

Rocky, Jocky, Pocky and Cocky
played Come Clean! with Arlene, Marlene
and Josephine

Wacky, Lacky, Tacky and Macky
played Upside Down Cake with Adina, Marina
and Robertina

MILITARY HISTORY

When they sent in the Old 69th ('The Muffdivers')
they defeated the Amazons in a few short skirmishes.

TO BE SNIFFED AT

If young men are sniffing
at the thought of women,
this is like a stallion
pawing lustful ground.
The sniffs you hear from old men
are far more disbelieving,
it's a disillusioned
non-admiring sound.

THE DEFEATED HUSBAND

For breakfast I had
                an egg and bad temper

For lunch I had
                a herring and bad temper

For tea I had
                tea and bad temper

For dinner I had
                chicken and bad temper

THE ANTI-CEREBRAL GUT-REACTION POEM

Eh?
      Um?
Ah!
Oh!
Oo!
      Ugh!
      Yuk!
Pow!
WAM!
ZONK!
      AAAARGH!

EVE AND THE APPLE

A young girl whose life-style the malicious
described, loosely, as too meretricious,
said 'When the boys peel me
and delightfully feel me,
I just feel like a Golden Delicious!'

AUTUMN

Life is sad and so slow and so cold
as the leaves that were green turn to gold,
as the lonely lake fills
and there's ice in the hills
and the long loathly winter takes hold. . .

NIGHT SCENE

There's a slow tolling bell in the dark
as the keepers are closing the park.
Like a desert, it's bare;
and each tree and each chair
is a blurred indeterminate mark.

THE FATHER OF ENGLISH POETRY

Spade-bearded Geoffrey Chaucer
only rhymes with saucer –
a word that wasn't around
when everybody went for (and *everybody* went for)
        that marvellous Chaucer sound.

THE NOT EXACTLY HAIKUS

1 SOPHISTICATION

In the highly select brothels of the East
they are putting rouge on the lips of the vulva
to please the oil millionaires from the West.

2 SPECTRUM

On the bookshelf, as well as the *Collected Shorter
Poems of W. H. Auden*, we also find
The Sillier Poems of Sebastian Hairnet.

3 MIRACLE

As the preacher speaks loud against lust
the hard erect penis of God storms out of a cloud
and beats him into the earth.

4 TUDOR

Then Margery Mylkeducke
her kyrtle shee didde uptucke,
looking forwarde to a fucke.

5 SUCCESS

A lunatic who thinks he's living in the Nineties
writes a book of Stevensonian essays:
In Pudendis Muliebribus. Everyone is ravished.

6 HAIKUS

Anything sufficiently short and solemn
or portentously trivial
will be much admired by many.

POWER POLITICS

When it's only a girl on a bicycle
we cross even though the lights are against us.
If she were a bus or a horde of cars
our feet would falter.

THE SEXUAL SIGH

The small buttocks of men, that excite the women. . .
but ah! the beautiful feminine broadness!

WHAT THE RICH CHILDREN IMAGINE

It's a bad life
for the poor children.
They're eating tabby cats
with kitten sauce.

HAIKU: THE TIME OF EAST/WEST COMPARISON

Madame Butterfly
marvelled at Pinkerton's big
cock (why she loved him).

ON THE AMBIVALENCE
OF MALE CONTACT SPORTS

Among men who play Rugger
you seldom find a bugger –
nobody strokes a bum
in the scrum.
Nevertheless. . .

A REMARKABLE THING

A remarkable thing about wine,
which we drunkards and lechers all bless so,
is the way it makes girls look more fine –
but ourselves, on the contrary, less so.

THE EDGE ON US

At the Chelsea wedding
the accents are so high, sharp and bright
you could cut the cake with them!

CONSEQUENCES

When Dr Feelingverse
met Miss Woodright
at the Literal Centre,
he said to her
'Your feet are uneven';
she said to him
'Keep your dactyls to yourself!'
and the result was
a litter of blind poems.

A DULL MORNING ENLIVENED

On a dull morning
a student brings me a poem
comparing her husband's cock to an aubergine.
I think: this is more like it!

AMERICANS

Americans have very small vocabularies.
They don't understand words like 'constabularies'.
If you went up to a cop in New York and said
'I perceive you are indigenous!' he would hit you on
     the head.

TRANSFORMATION

It's sad when girlfriends turn into wives,
and wives turn into housewives – lust
flies out of the window. It isn't 'Bite me again!'
but 'Don't sit in *that* chair – it causes dust!'

AN EMBLEM OF GOVERNMENT
(ELIZABETHAN)

All your bookshop assistants
are notable stealers of books.

EDUCATION
(LORD LEATHERHEAD'S SONG)

Nobody ever can call me a fool,
because I once went to that Eton School.
No one can say that I'm backward at knowledge,
because I once went to the old Eton College.

HAIKU: THE SEX WAR

Foreskin-flensing Jews,
clitoricidal Arabs,
are locked in conflict.

FOUND IN V. S. PRITCHETT

How, Rachel asked, did the raw young man come to
    be
married to Sonia, an actress at the top of the tree,
fifteen years older than he?
'The old girl knew her,' he said; 'she
was his mother's friend.'
                          – *Did You Invite Me?*

BLACK CLERIHEW

President Amin
demanded sex with the Queen
as the price for releasing the British
(he was feeling remarkably skittish).

INK

The ink of the love letters is dry,

and that's as much as to say
that the sperm that flows between the lovers
is also dry.

History, like the bones of the dinosaurs,
is always dry.

L. O. V. E.

A sadist sent a masochist a letter.
It said: 'Slave, I demand your presence! Quick!'
On the envelope was S.W.A.L.K.
(Sealed With A Loving Kick).

A PRONOUNCED DIFFERENCE

The simple villagers on the Meuse
in their ignorance speak of a *masseuse*.
Bellowing confident, like a moose,
the Americans call her a massoose.

THE SHORT BLAKE-STYLE
GNOMIC EPIGRAM

A voice was heard from a bottle of hock,
saying:
I am the ghost of W. H. Auden's cock!

AFTER DEATH

They say Death's perfect Peace and Rest. That's
    interesting.
But if we don't have consciousness, how shall we
    know we're resting?

DARK CONSOLATION

Even the little battered baby,
as it lies dying in its cot,
has known moments of happiness.

JULIA WOOD

If Julia Wood, if only Julia Wood!
I know, by instinct, it would be so good!
If only, only, Julia, Julia Wood!

Ah, but Wood Julia? I think Julia Wood
if I approached her gently – as I cood –
for Julia's not a babe in any Wood;

yes, I believe that Julia truly Wood,
she's not fictitious like Red Riding Hood.
Julia Wood like to! I'm sure Julia Wood!

NATURAL ENEMIES

The last people to be sentimental about cats
will be the mice.
The last people to honour the memory of Churchill
will be the miners.

IMAGE

A girl is
idly
flicking a
lighter
making it
come

A MEMORY OF 1953

I swear by all the rules of evidence, the timekeepers
    and the clocks,
that at a Boat Race Party I heard a girl seriously say:
'You can always tell the Oxford crew, they're the ones
    with the dark blue cox.'

THE FULLERS

And among those masterly poems, some are
    schoolmasterly too.

THE INDIAN LOVE LYRIC

Her rose is open.
It flowers with love.

Her black hair binds me.

If that rose closes
part of me will die.

CARD PLAY
(folk poem)

Lay the King of Cads
on the Queen of Whores,
set the Five of Dogs
on the Knave of Thieves,
place the Two of Hands
on the Two of Tits
and the Four of Legs
on the Ace of Beds.

Put the Three of Dreams
by the Queen of Love,
take the Ten of Toes
from the King of Knives,
from the Eight of Fingers
move the Two of Thumbs
be ready for Good Luck
when it comes.

HAIKU OF FEMALE OLD AGE

Many old women
are like empty paper bags,
with that crumpled look.

THE BASIC DESIRES

I want to drill a hole in your chicken

pull your rabbits to pieces

manipulate your guinea-pigs

destroy your pets for ever

LE PETIT POÈME FRANÇAIS

Hélas pour ces froids *gentlemen* anglais
        (avec leurs femmes laides),
dont tous les membres (sauf que le membre viril)
        sont absolument raides!

INSULTS TO THE BRAIN

In 1948 somebody told me
about Dylan Thomas's behaviour in The Gargoyle,
how he would go round the room on all fours
begging at the tables, like a dog, for a drink.

'Little Dylan wants a little drinkie!'

Good for a laugh – from the unsympathetic
or the envious other poets
or the professional disrupters, who think it's funny
to ring strangers on a Sunday morning
screaming 'Quarter to seven! Time to get up!'

But what (besides alcohol – the direct cause)
made him do it?
That is very far from a laughing matter.

Part II

MORE LITTLE ONES

TO MARGO

In life's rough-and-tumble
you're the crumble on my apple crumble
and the fairy on my Christmas tree!
In life's death-and-duty
you've the beauty of the Beast's own Beauty –
I feel humble as a bumble-bee!

In life's darkening duel
I'm the lighter, you're the lighter fuel –
and the tide that sways my inland sea!
In life's meet-and-muster
you've the lustre of a diamond cluster –
a blockbuster – just a duster, me!

CLEARING THE DESK

Just a minute while I throw this badger
out through the window, squash a few squirrels,
blow up a pig, shoot some bloody hawks,
eliminate the bats and tortoises,
crucify all crows,
pulverise a pike, make the owls into omelettes,
dig a grave for the ground-hog!

Now I am ready to write.

A POSSIBLE LINE OF WILLIAM EMPSON

A tie, in dining cars, commands respect

A POSSIBLE LINE OF ALFRED, LORD TENNYSON

The rhododendrons at the end of June

A POSSIBLE LINE OF JOHN CLARE

The little tittlemouse goes twiddling by

SEASONAL TRIPLE HAIKU:
THE TOURIST SEASON

From Santa Croce,
into the warm piazza,
they pour. A blonde asks:

'Where's the bathroom?' She
bugs the Italian guide.
He remains charming.

Another woman
says: 'They sure were a power–
ful bunch of artists!'

AN EXETER RIDDLE

Sitters on the mead-bench,   quaffing among
       questions,
I saw a thing –   tell me its totality.
A boy sped by,   his feet did not grind gravel,
high was his head,   incautious in the company
of the might of mountains   and a rock-rent liquid.
His hands moved little,   his legs seemed listless,
yet he woke the wind   and exacerbated echoes,
wending not to war   in a charging chariot,
unhelped by horses,   whirling like the wind.
Test-tube technology   covered him completely.
Seen for a second,   he was gone ghostly
as though he had never been.   Vouchsafe me this
                                    vision!

THE DEATH OF A MOTHER

So pitiful and small, such skin-and-bone!

RELIGIONS OF THE ABSURD

What people believe
is often unbelievable.
That a virgin could conceive
is inconceivable!

HAIKU: LOCOMOTOR ATAXIA

Four steps. A long halt.
The old man has a poet's
bad creative block.

THE ATHEIST TYPOGRAPHER IN THEATRELAND

Outside *Jesus Christ Superstar*
it says how it's so long-running
and there's a quote from *The Times*
that calls it 'mind stunning' –
but that's a literal, it seems to me,
the second *n* should be a *t*.

LINES ON THE DEATH OF POPE PAUL VI BY E. J. THRIBB (17)

So. Farewell then
Pope Paul VI.
My friend Keith
is learning Italian.
He says VI stands for
Veterano Intrepido.

But at least
you weren't called
Sixtus the Fifth.
In the old days
Popes were confusing.

Keith's Mum
says you were holy.
She says holy men
are very good and make
pronouncements

about things of importance
to women, e.g. birth control.

Some said you
were infallible.

Personally
I find it hard to say
what I feel about you.
Keith says
750 million Catholics
can't be wrong.

THE MISSISSIPPI

I am Old Man Mississippi,
full of Time and Mud –
you all must be pretty nippy
if I ever flood!
Swim in me? You would be dippy!
Foolish flesh and blood
would end woeful, dead and drippy!
Keep your distance, bud!

SEAMUS HEANEY

He's very popular among his mates.
I think I'm Auden. He thinks he's Yeats.

THE CRIMINAL CODE

Just one God, right? For me and you
it's God next door, the mate of Stew.
Football we know, we've been to Craven
Cottage – but what's an 'image' and what's 'graven'?
We swear all right, in court and out –
there'd be no fucking life without.
Church? What a hole, like in the head!
All *we* want from a church is lead.
Honouring parents? Likely lads
think nothing's squarer than their Dads.
Don't kill on jobs – unless it's plain
they'd recognise your lot again.
You're joking, surely? Thought you knew,
kids can commit adultery too.
Write it on walls: THOU SHALT NOT SQUEAL
(for us there's no such word as 'steal')
but if free pardons come your way,
then perjure, shop your mates, O.K.?

Don't know what 'covet' is. A man
must grab as much loot as he can.

NORTH LOVE

I never sycamores so sweet
as to behold the walls of York
and to patrol her dimpled feet
as lazy of the minster talk

so happy of the hard-won stone
her weight inevitable bears
a pinkness that is mine alone
and worshipping her tender ears

the lightness of a summer dress
I love some colour of her eyes
the more of me and she no less
whose beauty comes as no surprise

exacerbate the fingered hand
unspeakable the quiet hips
of love such charm as contraband
and not compared the shapely lips.

MOCK CHRISTMAS CAROL

Jesus Christ was born today!
Hooray, hooray, hooray, hooray!
Whatever any of you may say
He was born to cancel our terrible sins
And save us all from loony bins!
Hooray, hooray, hooray!

Jesus Christ was born today!
Hooray, hooray, hooray, hooray!
This is no time to watch and pray,
Let's all get drunk and drink a toast
To the Virgin Mary and the Holy Ghost!
Hooray, hooray, hooray!

Jesus Christ was born today!
Hooray, hooray, hooray, hooray!
Over-eating's a lovely way
To do Him honour; each Yuletide gift
Gives Him a God Almighty lift!
Hooray, hooray, hooray!

HAIKU: THE WIT AND WISDOM
OF CYRIL CONNOLLY

Connolly called the
British 'sheep with a nasty
side'. How very true!

A TITLED LADY

At once a picture comes into my mind of a stately
beauty, topless perhaps, being manoeuvred into a
                                        ballroom
by a burly footman. He walks slowly backwards,
                                        firmly
grasping one of her excited nipples in each white-
                                gloved hand.

HISTORY

Ensuing events impede the backward view.

CRICKET, LOVELY CRICKET!

It's an experimental congruence!
It's a probationary similarity!
It's a proving lucifer!
It's an investigatory rapport!
It's a probing likeness!
It's a dry-run flamethrower!
It's a try-out igniter!
It's a fact-finding similitude!
It's a researchful correspondence!
It's a trial contest!
It's a Test Match!

VARIATION ON A THEME OF WILLIAM BLAKE: AMBITIONS OF YOUNG WOMEN

Some girls long to influence men's hearts
but others concentrate on other
equally private parts.

ON READING THE POEMS OF MATTHEW PRIOR TO AN AUDIENCE OF ONE AT THE POETRY SOCIETY

It was one of a series called *Celebrations*.
One Scotsman, a teetotaller, turned up.

I felt sorry for Prior, an admired poet in his day,
and in my opinion as good as Dryden (much funnier).

I read for an hour, sipping whisky and water.
Afterwards I took the audience to a pub, he drank
        lemonade.

Was this a reflection on my reading or the Philistines
        of London?
I prefer to think Prior was far too good for them.

DAISY ASHFORD
(born 1881. *The Young Visiters* written 1890, published 1919)

Lords worshipped like the Deity
by the laity!
They must have thought Rothermere
was rather mere.
They had such innocence!
The inner sense
of nine-year-old simplicity
had authenticity,
each well-got-up dainty feeder knew
what Ouida knew:
you only looked quite the thing
if a Duke gave you a ring.

HAIKU: WOMEN IN WARTIME

Every small arms
instructor knew they had a
cut-away portion.

ROBERT GRAVES

A remarkable poet is Graves –
he throws out far more than he saves!
Each time he's Collected
huge chunks are rejected!
Yes, it's true – that's the way *he* behaves!

SELF-ADULATION

There's a foul smell, like pilchards left untinned,
where Rowse, the Cornish Shakespeare, breaks his
    wind.

IN A LONDON BOOKSHOP

There's a Scots poet called Dunbar –
they looked at me as from afar –
he wrote love poems, and divine,
a master of the lovely line –
they looked askance, they looked as though
they didn't really want to know –
he knew the Court, the field, the meadow,
'Twa Mariit Wemen and the Wedo',
satires and dirges, never loth,
he used his genius on them both –
they pursed their lips in noble scorn –
among the finest ever born,
he was far superior to
the poets sold in stacks by you –
they spoke as proud as pigs in bran:
We've never 'eard of such a man.

IN THE LAND OF VOWEL-REVERSED RHYMING

Now strippers everywhere flaunt their white loins
in King's Arms, Dukes and Bulls and the White
    Lions –
full in the face, to Puritans, vitriol
but welcome to the tillers of the soil
(Scots granite to the Western clay, lias),
who love to watch them wriggle on the dais.
From mountain crofts and flat alluvial plains,
the Dais and Hodges, Micks and Joes and Ians,
combine with Rams, Aquarians and Leos
to worship birds and bushes, tits and toes.

MOZART

Mozart
had all the skill that denotes Art –
his scores totalled milliards
when he was playing billiards.

NOT WAVELL BUT BROWNING

Nobody read him, the poor sod,
He was always moaning:
I am much more way out than you think
And not Wavell but Browning.

Poor chap, he always loved Larkin
And now he's dead,
The critics were too cold for him, his art gave way
They said.

Oh, no no no, they were too cold always
(He still never stopped moaning)
I was obscene and avant-garde and obscure
And not Wavell but Browning.

Note
Wavell was the British general of the Second World War who edited
a conservative anthology of English verse called *Other Men's Flowers*.
To the Victorians, Browning was the last word in newness and
incomprehensibility.

A VICTORIAN QUESTION

How could those crinolined ladies
flounce down on pisspots?

NORTH AMERICAN HAIKU

Hail, tribes of Outer
Alcoholia – the Rednose
and Goutfoot Indians!

BROKEN-RHYTHM HAIKU

Our cat
is the greatest thing on four legs
since Fred Astaire and Ginger Rogers.

AUSTRALIAN NOTE

It's not well known in leafy Pymble
that Malory called Pontremoli Point Tremble.

RESURRECTION

On the Last Day the wrecks will surface all over the
    sea.

AT THE VILLA ROSE

The black shit of Hélène Vauquier.

FREE FOR ALL

In a Competition poem I read:
'If I am not a poet
why does my heart bleed?'
And I think to myself 'Quite!
Nobody ever seems to imagine
that a poet's a person who can actually *write*.'

ORGASMS OF THE LOWER CLASSES

And when they come they shout out loud
        'O Didcot!' and 'O Stroud!'
Or even cry 'O Mum!' 'O Dad!'
        'Wowee!' or 'What a lad!'
But ladies murmur 'What a pleasure!
I'm truly grateful, beyond measure!'

A POSSIBLE LINE OF MARY WILSON IN EARLY 1979

Oh, dear old Betjeman, please do not die!

MUSICAL ECHOES

Who could make, out of musical notes floating
like sunbeams and motes, art?

                                    Mozart.

Which composer of the British nation was
most unlikely to call a station *el gare*?

                                    Elgar.

Who, if a girl in the gardens of Spain said
Play that again! might defy her?

                                    De Falla.

Who wrote a *Bolero* with a theme that a fool
in a dream could unravel?

                                    Ravel.

Whose huge family tree (what a lark!) was
all musical, branch, twig and bark?

                                    Bach.

Who sometimes woke in the night with a scream,
it would seem, crying: *Marguerite is NOT all
sticky with sentimentality and covered in
goo! No!*

                                    Gounod.

A POSSIBLE LINE OF KIPLING, CONCERNING GEORGE MACBETH

He's a gentleman of Scotland, living South

AMBITION

I tell you frankly
I want to write a poem that is so moving
that it leaves all other poems standing.

I want the readers
to be queueing up like mourners when a Pope dies,
crying their eyes out, loving their emotion,

I want the actors
to dramatise it all over the BBC,
misprints and all, in love and sorrow,

I want it to be
a statutory legend in its lifetime,
built to outstare the twittering birdlike critics.

RURAL RHYMES

I know that God made badgers all
And blessed each hawthorn by the way.
Each animal, however small,
Is there to teach us how to pray,
And every little hedgerow flower
Bears silent witness to His power.

There is a blessing in the rain,
As it descends on me and you,
And in the ripening of the grain
We all can see God's purpose too –
Ah! no escape! We flee, we run,
But He shines o'er us like the sun!

PART OF A LEGEND

Sir Launchalot sails his small pinnace on the Lake of
  Love.

CHILDREN'S BOOKS

When you read a line like:
They all took a Day Return to Pigglepopkin
you know you're reading a children's book.
Without funny names children's books could not exist.

'13 DIE AS COPTER DITCHES IN THE SEA'

13 die as copter ditches in the sea –
   and all the rhythm's broken.
This is the death of our technology –
13 die as copter ditches in the sea,
the printing presses whirr a threnody,
   technical details. No last word was spoken.
13 die as copter ditches in the sea,
   and all the rhythm's broken.

MARTIAL ARTS

1. *Good*

Avidus, greedy for praise, is a good fellow,
he's good at drinking with the reviewers –
no wonder they call his poetry good too!

2. *A Name*

That nobody Shaxberd, whose name nobody seemed
    able to spell
and who lived almost unknown in his lifetime,
has done an infinite amount of harm.

By giving hope to so many thousands of bad neglected
    poets.

3. *Virago*

Agrippinilla lives in California.
She's well into Cunt Positive
and proud of her bullet-shaped clitoris.

TRIOLET: BUYING RECORDS IN JULY

I've purchased *The Ring*,
I shall play it this winter,

a long-drawn-out thing,
I've purchased *The Ring*

where for hours they all sing,
it's not cryptic like Pinter.

I've purchased *The Ring*.
I shall play it this winter.

BILLY BUDD

The sailorboys all gave a cheer
for their Captain, that old 'Starry' Vere –
he was the bugger
in charge of the lugger
and incontrovertibly queer.

TRIOLET: WINE IN OLD AGE

The old men ballet round the loo
and rise, in turn, from drinking wine.

This is a thing they have to do.
The old men ballet round the loo.

It's like a dance, it's like a queue.
Though bladders weaken, they feel fine.

The old men ballet round the loo
and rise, in turn, from drinking wine.

ALCOHOL

Oh, so slowly the brain starts to go
as the cells are burned out, row by row,
and they're never replaced –
so we're certainly faced
with oblivion – the last thing we know!

TOURIST TRAFFIC

If you're in the market for fucks or
a girl or a boy who just sucks or
desire an Egyptian
of any description –
get going on a slow boat to Luxor.

D.T.

Dylan Thomas was rotund
and orotund
with the voice of a portwine parson.

CHORUS OF A KIPLING-STYLE POEM
ABOUT TEENAGE VIOLENCE TO PARENTS

So it's
    a strong straight left for the Mum you love
and a hefty kick for her arthritic hip!
    It's the iron hand in the iron glove
and some knives of different sizes to give Dad some
    nice surprises
and the black eye and the swollen lip!

DER HÖLLE RACHE KOCHT IN MEINEM
HERZEN!

(Hell's revenge is cooking in my heart!)
                      – *Die Zauberflöte* (Schikaneder/Mozart)
The Grigsons are a team. They do very well.
Jane does the cooking. Geoffrey gives us hell.

THE HIGHBROW HANGOVER

Today I am feeling subfusc
and as brittle and brusque as a rusk,
most frighteningly friable –
no action is viable –
not a man nor a mouse but a husk!

FOOD FOR THOUGHT

Munchester! Stockpot!
In a train you can eat England!

ANCIENT WISDOM

The Myths are there for micky-taking.
The High Streets are there for money-making.

The Wars are there for killing people,
Old Age to make the strong ones feeble.

Sex is there to bring on babies
and give gay dogs the barking rabies.

Life is there to irritate us
and make us feel our lack of status.

DOUBLE HAIKU: SEXISM

All the tall thin gay
solicitors tell their boy
friends how women are,

without exception,
about three feet tall at most,
with big smelly cunts.

A VERY WISE REMARK
MADE BY HARRY COLLIER
AT CAMBRIDGE UNIVERSITY IN 1935

Why does a publican have a large belly
and his wife an enormous bust?
There's a reason, my acute friend said.
They fit like jigsaw pieces in that *mêlée*
occasioned by conjugal lust,
when they're locked together in bed!

SAUCE FOR THE GOOSE

To hate being a sex object? All very well and good –
and perhaps some men's desires are a bit mean and
    shoddy.
But when has anyone been thrown out of the
    sisterhood
for lusting after another woman's body?

VIOLENT PASSIONS

The mouth can be quite nasty in a bite
The lover's pinch can be malicious too
Legs kick, as well as tangle, in a bed

Words can be harsh and not console or rhyme
Fighting is also love's especial food
Hands can enlace with hands or round a neck

The tools that pierce can be unyielding steel
Attractive nails can score, like claws, the face
Fingers can spread on cheeks, harmful and strong

Hair can be pulled in war, that's stroked in peace
The fighting female differs from the male
The spitting cat attacks the barking dog

WHO IS CIRCE?

Who is Circe? what is she,
That all these swine commend her?
Sexy, bald, and drunk is she;
The Devil such force did lend her.
Underneath the Upas Tree
All the fiends attend her.

WELTANSCHAUUNG

If you look at the world, it looks bad!
And this can make some people sad.
The slightly demented
are fairly contented,
the happiest ones are quite mad.

THE YOUNG POET IN
THE LITERARY WORLD

The big insensitive faces / come up to you at parties
and you are wondering
who that terrible-looking fat tart is,

and she turns out to be a / greatly revered novelist
and that old purple man
a Prize-Winning Poet – unless you're pissed.

The words may have been winning / but the flesh is
      weak;
like everyone's, it ages.
A profile like that of an Ancient Greek

is foxed so much more quickly / than the humble paper
that holds a masterpiece –
grave marks stain hands, all that kind of caper.

You think they should look noble? / but no, it doesn't
      follow.
Each is just the mould that
once formed the statue; and, like all moulds, they're
      hollow.

DIVORCED WOMEN IN DORMITORY TOWNS

The lives they travel in are like comfortable cars –
but they bore them. Oh, nothing happens!
With enough money and custody of the children,
do they sometimes regret the drunken husbands?

Lovers are hard to come by. Romance
in the brash shapes of feminine longing
left them twenty years ago. All that equipment
simply languishes unused in houses with gardens.

They are most like the day-trippers who drive
into safari parks. They're afraid to go out
into the world of lions. Claustrophobes,
they watch their sweet bodies shrivel like grapes.

MARTIAL AND DOMITIAN
('The Book Of The Games')

In those days it wasn't keeping up with the Joneses –
it was keeping in with the Emperors.

If he held Games, you had to praise them.
After all, look what he provided!
The amphitheatre filled with water, for a real sea
    battle,
women killing lions on the dry sand,
a condemned criminal crucified *and* eaten by animals,
tigresses fighting lions, bears elephants,
a rhinoceros goring a bull like an old leather ball –
a genuine banquet of assorted cruelties.

How could anyone fail to praise an Emperor like that?

A LINE THAT MIGHT BE A STUMBLING BLOCK TO THE PURITAN FAITHFUL

The patriarchs, with all their concubines

HAIKU: MRS X

An old police dog
sniffs my knickers. I charge him
£8,000. Wow!

HAIKU: THIRTY YEARS AGO

I climbed up her white
redbushed body. She had big
green eyes like a cat's.

HAIKU: FOREPLAY

Undressing, she laugh-
ingly hung her panties on
his hard hatrack cock.

REPUTATIONS

Poets are very touchy. They have to be the greatest.
Or (if not quite *that*) at least the latest.

A HAIR OF THE DOGGEREL

It's so unfair that alcohol makes you fat
and feel, next day, like a half-dead bat.
The Devil's at the bottom of this, it's understood, for
    you
would expect something so nice
to be terribly good for you.

THE SAD WIDOW

Candy-floss Blackpool, wet and windy, with the
     sadness
of the sad sad widow
Pier and ballroom, hotel bar window, with the sadness
of the sad sad candy
Flossy sea-spray, wrought iron, whelk-smell, with the
     sadness
of the sad sad Blackpool
Popping brown seaweed, chip shops, windy, with the
     sadness
of the sad sad widow

Blackpool, rock pool, boarders, sandworms, with the
     sadness
of the sad sad widow
Thin landladies, thin-sliced bacon, with the sadness
of the sad sad wetness
Sea wind, raincoats, crab claws, windblown, with the
     sadness
of the sad sad floss-stick
Ballroom, bar-room, bright lights, rainstorms, with the
     sadness
of the sad sad widow

Note
This was written on a course at the Arvon Foundation, Totleigh
Barton, as a poem-game. Two or three students, improvising, act a
short piece on a theme dictated by another student. Spurred or
inspired by this, all present then have 12 minutes in which to write
a poem on some aspect of what has been performed.

IN AUSTRIA

When you drink a *Qualitätswein*
you will never be a loser –
this just means the wine is fine
for the fairly choosy boozer.

When the *Bestattungsunternehmer*
takes the butcher and the baker
he is not a loud proclaimer
but a quiet undertaker.

Brandteigschokoladencremekrapfen –
pronounce it, you will make mistakes!
But nothing terrible will hapfen,
these are simply chocolate cakes!

SPRING SONG

Lovers are rolling over like cats in the sunshine,
allowing their tummies to be tickled,
licking one another,

full of the excitement of finding a new person,
happy in the warm emotion.
The questions come later.

Soon they will discover there are two different people
involved in these affairs; quite simply,
spring is never summer.

HAIKU: CULTURE

Ah, wee-wee! The great
French writers: Rubberlegs and
Ballsache and Racing!

PANTOUM: WORSHIP

So much I deify your glorious globes
(and kiss your round re-entrants and your cleft –
the Oriental earrings in your lobes
are all you wear) I touch both right and left

and kiss. Your round re-entrants and your cleft!
On your white skin the blacks of body hair
are all you wear (I touch). Both right and left
I see a Heaven feminine and fair,

on your white skin the blacks of body hair,
where both shine with a single, sexual light.
I see a Heaven feminine and fair
that overwhelms me now – it is so bright

where both shine with a single, sexual light,
the two, the privileged, that make the love!
That overwhelms me. Now, it is so bright –
yet comforting, the finger in the glove,

the two, the privileged, that make the love
(the Oriental earrings in your lobes),
yet comforting (the finger in the glove).
So much I deify your glorious globes!

SEPTEMBER

It's warm and it's wet in September
as the summer burns down to an ember –
but the cold weather comes,
freezing toes, tits and bums,
in the two months that follow December.

IN MEMORIAM

Like grim death, we say. A grinning death
gets painted on black leather.

Not for these. Three tourist motorbikes
with right of way on unknown French roads.

One looks back. He wavers
into oncoming traffic.

Notifying. Taking the body home.
Telling the parents.

Not work for twenty-year-olds.
Or seeing it.

Hardest of all, accepting it.
Accepting it.

MUSHROOM-SHAPED HAIKU:
IN A SEASON OF DESPAIR

We think, as we look
at our children: is this the
last generation?

TRIPLE HAIKU: MEASURE FOR MEASURE

Measure for Measure
has three creepy characters –
Angelo, the Duke,

Isabella. Why
does he abdicate? Simply
to test Angelo?

And why does she *not*
scream *Vows*! *Virginity*! when
he offers marriage?

BELGRADE

The two big rivers neighbour in the North

The early morning trams are suffering elephants

The sliding doors cremate the airport baggage

The tourist blouse can cost a whole week's pay

The spice is hidden, deeply, in the meat

The plums are resurrected in hard juice

The alphabet rejoices, two-in-one

CHASTITY IN BLOOMSBURY

Virginia was right in a way
to keep Leonard Woolf so at bay –
though she lifted her vest
for her V. Sackville-West,
that was only in amorous play!

A PERSON

She's mean and full of minge-water.

COMPETITION PIECE

There was a young lady of Leicester
whose boyfriends all fondly caressed her.
They squeezed both her boobs
like toothpaste in tubes
and then went ahead and undressed her.

A POSSIBLE LINE OF DR SAMUEL JOHNSON

The Pious Reasoner his Tear withholds.

Part III

EXTRA
LITTLE ONES

FOUND HAIKU: WATERLOO STATION GENTS

I want to whip the
bare bottom of a pretty
girl tied up for it.

ENGLAND AT CHRISTMAS, 1982

O silly little, proud and silly, country
so good at ceremonial, limited wars,
football (occasionally)! Snob Billy Buntery
gives all the rich, rich presents – Santa Claus
has handed out the land. He hates the serfs,
the common people, so uncommonly low;
loves dogs, cats, hunting, cricket, the green turfs
that make a stately-homely postcard show –
quite beautiful, memorials to old greed,
when what there was to take, to steal, to pinch
went to the bastard Baron on his steed
or landowners, enclosing each square inch,

or City men, who raise a joyous anthem
for a fake-lady bossyboots from Grantham.

DENIS

The perfect marriage, it must seem!
This is an advertising dream.

Where he is, he doesn't know.
Saatchi & Saatchi made him go!

To countries sad, or gay, or sinister.
He has to sit with the Prime Minister.

Dazed and dining, day and night,
he's not allowed out of her sight.

At all banquets there's a place
for his long square tortoise face.

Saatchi & Saatchi! We adore!
But they've a lot to answer for.

DOGS IN POLITE SOCIETY

Dogs always go for the loins of a guest
and sniff them with zest –
this embarrasses the rest.

THE LEIPZIG GEWANDHAUS ORCHESTRA GIVES PETER PORTER A STANDING OVATION

H ail, hail, Antipodean Promoter of Bach,
E xcellent verisimilitudinous versifier!
I n truth His Fugues are never too *einfach* –
L ate homage, though, they rightly must inspire!

P oet, preserve your civilising mission!
E xhalt High Art (the paint, the note, the word),
T hat may all end with our next nuclear fission –
E asy indeed to think such tasks absurd!
R anged against you, the forces of the market

P ropagate Pop, Free Verse, the slack, the sillies –
O that huge Juggernaut, tell them to park it
R ight up the Snowy River! Tell hillbillies
T hat His Chorales are rousing as hard liquor!
E xhort those high-born twits in Jags to nark it!
R evive the flame that's now a fitful flicker!

HAIKU: A SELF-DECEIVER

He's been in the same
room with Eliot, Pound, Yeats. *So*
he's a great poet!

CINQUAIN

Cinquains
are just silly
little pointless poems –
invented by Adelaide M.
Crapsey!

(Syllables in each line: 2/4/6/8/2)

SEXTET

The sextet is more of
a whimper than a
bang – it's designed
to have a
dying
fall.

(Invented by Gavin Ewart. Syllables: 6/5/4/3/2/1)

RURAL LIFE
(Rough Cider)

Down in Barton Sunshade
They don't drink lemonade
And the lads have hairy great enormous balls –
Every rip-roaring bugger
Is first-class at rugger,
As they come in the rucks and the mauls!

Down in Causley Betjers
The lasses love the lechers –
The pride of pricks that make their pussies pout –
They don't think it's a sin
When partners put it in,
The sin, for them, is when they pull it out!

A WELL-KNOWN LEADER OF THE WOMEN'S MOVEMENT GOES MAD AND WRITES A HYMN TO THE PENIS

O Penis, glorious Penis,
I love to see Thee rise,
to peer up to Thy pink-tipped top,
it seems to reach the skies!
I lie and worship vainly
or fall upon my knees,
Thy testicles make Three-in-One,
blest Trinity of threes!

DOUBLE HAIKU: S. C. U. M. *

Our society
doesn't need one for Cutting
Up Women. It does

that already in
several ways, and very
efficiently too.

* Society for Cutting Up Men (an American feminist organisation)

HAIKU: RUGGER

The fly-half jinks through
like a Cabbage White zigging
clear past cabbages.

THE ECLECTIC CHAIR

He's sitting in the Death Seat in *The George*
and Lethe clogs his brain with silt and sedge.

If anything now rises, it's his gorge;

his mind was once a bright and Blakean forge –

now drained as animals the butchers porge –
sees little, hears as much. He's on the edge,

he's sitting in the Death Seat in The George
and Lethe clogs his brain with silt and sedge.

Note
The 'Death Seat' in the BBC pub, The George, is by the door, on
the left as you go in. This is where the oldest BBC men sit before
they die. Lethe is of course the river of forgetfulness that encircles
the classical underworld. To 'porge' is to render an animal ritually
clean according to the Jewish faith.

KIPLINGESQUE: GOING WEST

When you see things hazy or not at all,
    Not even the oculist's card,
When at every step you're afraid you'll fall
And you have to hold on to a stick (or a wall)
    And reading is far too hard;
When the traffic slides by with a noise like mice
And everything must be repeated twice
And your friends all die and you feel depressed,
Why, then you will know (if you haven't guessed)
You're very quickly going West!

VARIATION ON TWO LINES OF W. B. YEATS

Love is staying for a bit
in the place of piss and shit.

A TRUE STORY OF A YOUNG WOMAN
IN THE FIFTIES

She lay on a towel sunbathing
on a genteel English beach.

A small brown dachshund rushed up to her
and began to make enthusiastic love to her arm.

She could do nothing about it. She was a lady.
In that world of ladies such things were not
    acknowledged.

She couldn't even shout (which would have been
    appropriate):
Fuck off!

When he had finished
she tripped down to the sea and washed the guilt off.

THE OLD COUPLES
(For Edward and Edwina*)

Of course they realise
there isn't much time left –
one old partner will soon be bereaved and bereft –

one day a sun will rise
that finds only one in the bed –
because the other one has been taken away, dead.

Proverbs and old saws
bear witness a thousand times
to this – so do all clocks and church chimes,

it's one of Nature's Laws,
but as it happens to me and you
it's always going to strike us as something new.

Gather ye rosebuds
or *Live well* say the bores
who are always sermonising the drunks and whores,

and some days *have* been duds. . .
with Death and Time on the brain,
we should make the most of the ones that remain.

* Edward and Edwina are two Edward Gorey toy cats, purchased
from the Gotham Book Mart, that sleep on our double bed.

WHAT A SURPRISE!

How amazing – there are Communists in the Unions!
How unbelievable – there are Fascists in the
    Boardrooms!

OGDEN NASH IN NAPLES

The favours of the girls of Naples
are not to be purchased with small items of office
                equipment, such as paperclips or staples.
Oh, no! They're much dearer.
They cost several thousand lire.

A JEWISH BEAUTY TO HER ADMIRERS

If you would earn my true respect,
kill any old Arab, of any old sect!

HAIKU: A NOTED DINOSAUR

Rhamphorhynchus has
a name like a character
found in *Aida*.

DRINKING SONG

Elated by the Great Depressant,
I was feeling fine.
Bottle, glass and lip – incessant
was the flow of wine!
Why on earth should people stop?
Drink it down to the last drop!

Ah, but wines have lees and dregs too,
they can turn the brain,
easily knock you off your legs too,
drive you quite insane,
there's an end to all the jokes
in the heart attacks and strokes!

PART OF A BORN-AGAIN TRIOLET COMES THROUGH THE POST

I am writing to tell you about the Good News of God's
    Kingdom.
We are all looking forward with the hope of a happier future.
I once saw a book about India, it was called 'The Land
    Of The Lingam'.
I am writing to tell you about the Good News of God's
    Kingdom,
and everyone in Woodborough Road and Australia
    thinks it will be fair dinkum –
though the World is falling apart, the Great Surgeon
    will perform a suture.
I am writing to tell you about the Good News of God's
    Kingdom.
We are all looking forward with the hope of a happier future.

Note
The first two lines are the beginning of a letter received by the
author on 24 April 1984, from an address in Woodborough Road,
Putney.

THE JEWEL IN THE CROWN

The best character is Mildred –
always drinking gin and getting fucked
and being nasty to everybody. . .
very proper reactions
to the Imperial situation!

SHOUTED OUT BY THE CHOIR
AT THE WEDDING

She's a willing wife,
a cuddlecomekin!
Her contours are convenient!

He's a penile pillar
of wildfire by night,
a masculine mainstay!

DRAWBACKS OF BEING A WOMAN

All girls can walk through a lavatory door –
but it's harder for them to pee on the floor!

Note
'Lavatory' = 'toilet' in the vernacular, and 'bathroom' in America.

BRIDGING APARTHEID
WITH RUGGER FIENDS

If the Devil himself
came up from Hell,
with fourteen other devils,
and said:
'I'm a red-hot practising bugger –
but I'm willing to play Rugger!'
they'd play Rugger!

DOUBLE HAIKU: DE GROOT
(Son of a musician and fellow-conscript, East Surreys,
    1940)

In the latrines, some-
one had written: DE GROOT IS
A CUNT. Next to this

somebody else had
written (more harshly): DE GROOT
IS A DOUBLE CUNT.

A NEVER-NEVER SLOGAN

Get stoned – with Stone's Ginger Wine!

FROM 'THE ATHEIST'S HANDBOOK'

I'd sooner put my trust in a drunken dentist than in
    God.

BREAKING OUT

So many little neatly tied lyrics!
Can you blame us if we go
for the poems that are mad, bad and dangerous to
    know!

OUT OF THE MOUTHS OF BABES AND FUCKLINGS

In a train from Southampton to Waterloo:
two young men, two young women, two babies –
one in arms, one in a carrycot.
Laughter, and 'fucking' the most popular adjective –
one of the men even called his girl a 'cunt'. . .
surely those babies will inherit a sophisticated
vocabulary!

NATURE IN THE RAW

The squeak of a hostess
as she sees, over your shoulder,
a more important guest arriving. . .

The squeak of the caterpillar
of the Death's Head Hawk Moth. . .

CELTIC TWILIGHTS

Dublin and Edinburgh are just the same –
and whisk(e)y-drinking's the only game!

102

A PSEUDO-LAUREATE GETS STARTED

(Notes on the Queen, etc.)

The Queen is tiny
but her crown is shiny –
the Duke's not so bad,
he's a bit of a lad,
and so is Andy,
he's really randy,
like Christine Keeler
and Rice-Davies (Mandy).

17 July 1984

AN UNDERGROUND MOVEMENT

The Hooded Clitoris
sits in an arbour
with her friends
Urethra and Labia,
planning and plotting
the feminist books to be
published by Fabia & Fabia.

WILLIS AND BOTHAM: A PREP SCHOOL POEM BY BILL FRINDALL ('THE BEARDED WONDER')

Willibags and Bottibogs are two strong men,
They played for England again and again.
They did well against Ozzies, Pakis and Hindis* –
But they seldom succeeded against the West Indies!

* Hindi is a language but occasionally, according to the *OED*, can
be a person too.

HAIKU: A JAPANESE DRIED FLOWER AT A POETRY READING

Take a poet. Drop
him in alcohol. He'll ex-
pand in full colour!

THE DEATHS OF HORRIBLE PEOPLE: A PARTIAL CONSOLATION

When all is done and all is said,
the horrible people at last lie dead.
Reagan and Thatcher go into the blue
along with Hitler – but so do you!

2/LT. JOHN HEPBURN, R. A.

You sat in the arse of the aircraft, watching the flak.
You were lucky that, like a boomerang, you came
   back.
You came back with a gong, hero of night attack,
To your earthbound comrades in Air Defence, in Light
   Ack-Ack!

Note

John Hepburn (one of the sons of Anna Wickham) was attached to
an RAF Bomber Group from the 47th LAA Regiment for a month
or so in 1942. He flew as a tail-gunner in a Wellington, to observe
the effectiveness of German anti-aircraft gunnery – for which he
was awarded a DFC. John was by no means a standard Army
officer; riding a motorbike in Service Dress and black boots was
about the form. His first Battery Commander was called Major
Cheese. One day he was summoned to the Battery Office for a
reprimand.

Major Cheese: Mr Hepburn! When you left the Mess last night I
            saw you *stagger*!
2/Lt Hepburn: Of course I staggered, Sir. I was bloody drunk!

T. S. ELIOT AND EZRA POUND

Eliot loved the music halls
(and he probably loved pantos).
Pound took the rubbish out of *The Waste Land*
and put it all into the *Cantos*.

THE BEGINNING OF A VICTORIAN NOVEL

'Hot fuck!' cried Louisa disdainfully. 'Git outa here,
    you scumbag!'
Florence, Harriet and Octavia maintained silence,
    hidden as they were behind the door of the
    conservatory.

NOT PEACE BUT A SWORD

Mosque or temple, church or steeple,
religions are keenest
on killing people!

FOUND POEM IN A ROBERT GRAVES LETTER (TO KARL GAY) 14 APRIL 1965

My life at Deya was beginning to stink.
I had to get out and think.

HAIKU: G. M. HOPKINS

'I got a sudden revelation when I looked at the *facsimile* poem in
Desmond Flower's *English Poetic Autographs*: I exclaimed, aghast
at the handwriting, "That man bites his nails." "Yes," said Grete
(our tame-but-wild graphologist) "and has other comfort habits!" '
Robert Graves, letter to James and Mary Reeves

G. M. Hopkins? Could
it be Genital Massage?
It seems quite likely!

A MARTIAN HAIKU

Departure Boards at
Waterloo flick their packs like
impatient gamblers.

RUPERTA BEAR'S FEMINIST POEM

We live in a society that's phallocratic
but we're beginning to make literature cunnicentric.
Already many women can only read books by
     women –
if they accidentally read something written by a MAN
at once a horrible feeling comes over them,
the words grip them like the hands of a rapist,
with a scream they throw the book from them!

CHRISTOPHER HOGWOOD

Christopher Hogwood
plays the harpsichord better than a dog would.
You've probably heard
him worrying away at Byrd.

EXILES FROM THE SUN (BLAKE-STYLE)

Even in the streets of cold, wet Britain
the little West Indians can dance and sing!

TWO FOUND POEMS IN SIEGFRIED SASSOON'S DIARY
(1923–1925) p.197 and p.203

1. A weakness of mine
   is for sparkling red wine.

2. Drank half a bottle of Moselle
   and feel well.

VARIATIONS ON PEPYS, 2 SEPT. 1667*

Bab May and Lady Castlemaine
and all that wicked crew
are throwing their weight about again,
to fuck and buck and screw
and squirm into the King's regard
and urge him to do wrong –
who praise the hardness of his yard
and tell him it is long!

* 'and he is great with Bab May, my Lady Castlemaine, and that
  wicked crew'. Baptist May was the courtier who devoted
  himself to the pleasures of the King. Lady Castlemaine was the
  Senior Mistress, very given to political intrigue.

A BETJEMAN VARIATION
(Tune: 'Red Sails in the Sunset')

As hot as a hornet,
As warm as a wasp,
They're dying like flies in
The old Cottage Hosp!

1914

Rupert Brooke's young swimmers into cleanness
      leaping
landed in the mud and blood of the Western Front.

TRIOLET: UNSISTERLY BEHAVIOUR

It's the women are great willy-gigglers,
they will giggle at every mention!
Remembering beds! They were wrigglers!
It's the women are great willy-gigglers!
It's the comics sell jokes – they are higglers
and the willy-response their intention!
It's the women are great willy-gigglers,
they will giggle at every mention!

Note 'Higglers' are pedlars, travelling salesmen

BRIEF ENCOUNTERS

All beginning conversations
are fumbling through the clothes
towards the fornications
that pleasures these and those;

are they sometimes sad or serious
or frolicsome with fun –
delightful, deleterious?
Until the whole thing's done

you can never know the answer.
Is *she* quite what she seems?
Is *he* the Bengal Lancer
of her long erotic dreams?

Note
This is a twelve-minute poem, written as an exercise on a course
at Marylands College, Woburn.

READING

Paperbarks don't read paperbacks –
they're trees in Australia.
And to read a glossy magazine
you don't need glossolalia.

ALL MARRIAGES ARE MIXED

Did the Greeks have a word for it
(marital boredom)?
As every day they gazed at the same old face
from Samothrace?

ORDERING WHISKEY IN IRELAND

It's embarrassing to have to say
to a blonde-haired dyed barmaid:
Have you got a Black Bush?

CELTIC

The Irish are great talkers,
persuasive and disarming.
You can say lots and lots
against the Scots –
but at least they're never charming!

DECLINE AND FALL
(Evelyn Waugh)

For some lads it's always bad weather.
You could say that of Paul Pennyfeather.
Toffs, from Drinking Club rags,
Ran away with his bags –
He was sent down from Ox, hell for leather.

Then he taught in an awful Welsh school –
Prendy, Philbrick, cad Grimes (he's no fool).
Next it's prison – White Slaving
(Margot's face was worth saving??).
Ah, for her he was only a tool!

But he got back to Ox in the end
to drink cocoa with Stubbs, his old friend.

Note
This poem was written for a *New Statesman* Competition – fourteen
lines of verse, or less, to tell the story of a famous novel.

A SHAKESPEAREAN SONG

All around the distant tracks
motorbikes are farting,
whores are lying on their backs,
lovers' legs are parting.
Yo ho! Yo ho!
and all we know:
Ending is not starting.

In their glassy shining tanks
terrapins are twiddling,
buttoned bosoms on green banks
feel foul fingers fiddling.
Yo ho! Yo ho!
and all we know:
Life is fair to middling.

DYING

When the horrors of old age
gather round,
the most sensible thing you can do
is to die –
you may even get
Pie in the Sky.

And the preachers
are often heard
confidently to say
that Born Again Christians,
if there's a Holocaust,
will be swept up to Heaven
by angels
straightaway!

DEATH AND THE CHILD

Why dat man
poo poo?
Why dat man
bum bum?
Boy, dat man
dyin!

Why dat man
wee wee?
Why dat man
pee pee?
Boy, dat man
dyin!

Why dat man
come come?
Why dat man
toss toss?
Why, dat man
hanged, son!

THE WORLD OF GERALD HAMILTON

They're standing proud, those male parade-ground
 guardsmen,
so like toy soldiers, stiff, erect and red.
And so they'll be – for money magics guardsmen –
in any silken, scented Knightsbridge bed.

ORAL LOVE SONG

In days when I was barking up your canyon
 the echoes coming back were soft and sweet –
not like Chicago's North Side and O'Banion
 in 1924 – and I repeat
in days when I was barking up your canyon
 the echoes coming back were very sweet!

In days when I was occupied with rimming
 you seemed responsive to that near caress,
your joy quite overflowed, and I was swimming
 in oceans of your female happiness –
oh, yes! When I was occupied with rimming
 you seemed responsive to that near caress!

You were being served, and I was doing the plating,
 a waiter running to present each dish,
to bring you true delight, not keep you waiting,
 and pander to each taste and whim and wish –
oh, surely you were served, as I was plating,
 a waiter eager to present each dish!

THE LIFE AND THE WORK

All my life I've worked hard
(or fairly hard)
writing silly advertisements
or writing silly poems
by the yard,

making the new sows' ears from
a silk purse;
and all you have in the end is
a lot of old-style ads,
outdated verse.

Don't ever make the future
a sacred cow!
Believe me, all that really matters
is the problematical joy
of the here and now.

MY STOICISM

I can stand anything except pain –
and you can say that again!
When they start drilling my teeth
I know it's time for my friends
to send a wreath.

If, in the night, I ever get cramp
not even The Lady With The Lamp
could soothe that agony to an end
or cancel my thought that I'm going
right round the bend!

I'm also afraid that I'm going mad
(the critics would say *How sad*!)
but of course looniness might help
to stifle the terminal yelling,
the deathbed yelp!